MIND RIOT

COMING OF AGE IN COMIX

EDITED AND WITH AN INTRODUCTION BY **KAREN D. HIRSCH**
FOREWORD BY **PETER BAGGE**

ALADDIN PAPERBACKS

25 Years of Magical Reading

ALADDIN PAPERBACKS
EST. 1972

First Aladdin Paperbacks edition April 1997
Designed by Lily Malcom

Aladdin Paperbacks
An imprint of Simon & Schuster
Children's Publishing Division
1230 Avenue of the Americas
New York, NY 10020

Printed and bound in the United States of America
10 9 8 7 6 5 4 3 2 1

Library of Congress Cataloging-in-Publication Data
Mind riot : coming of age in comix / edited and with an introduction by Karen D. Hirsch ; foreword by Peter Bagge. — 1st Aladdin Paperbacks ed.
p. cm.
ISBN 0-689-80622-1 (alk. paper)
1. Youth—Conduct of life—Comic books, strips, etc. I. Hirsch, Karen D.
PN6726.M56   1997
741.5'973—dc21   96-48073
CIP

BBT 10/15/98 $9.99

TABLE OF CONTENTS

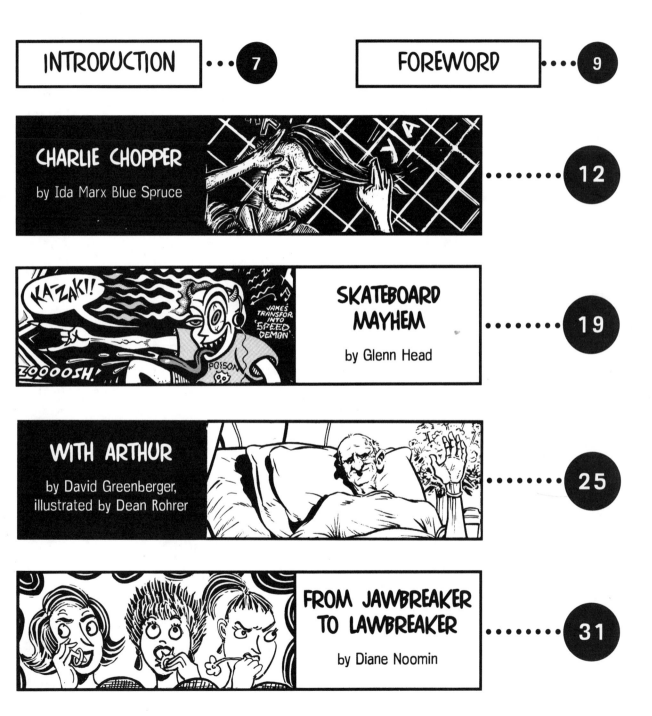

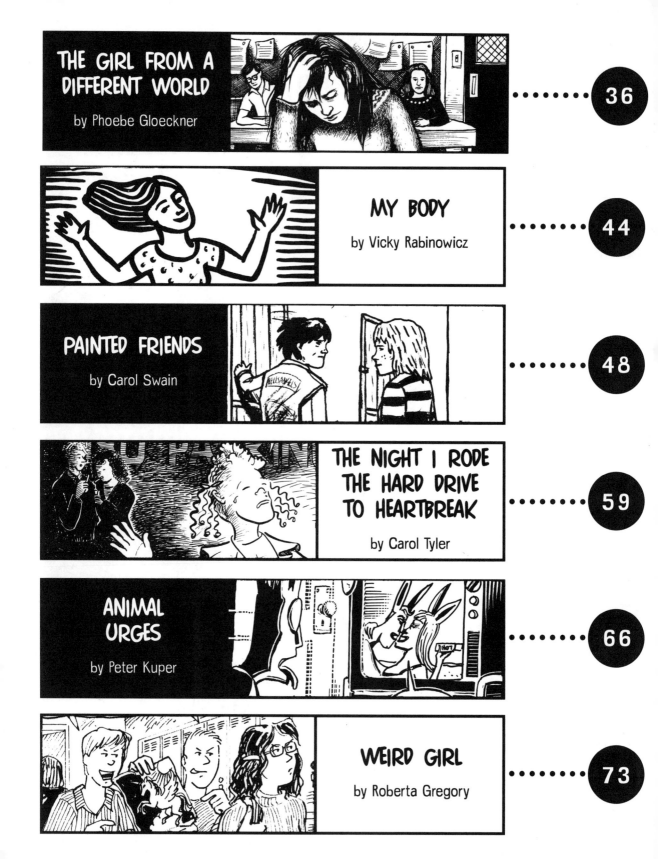

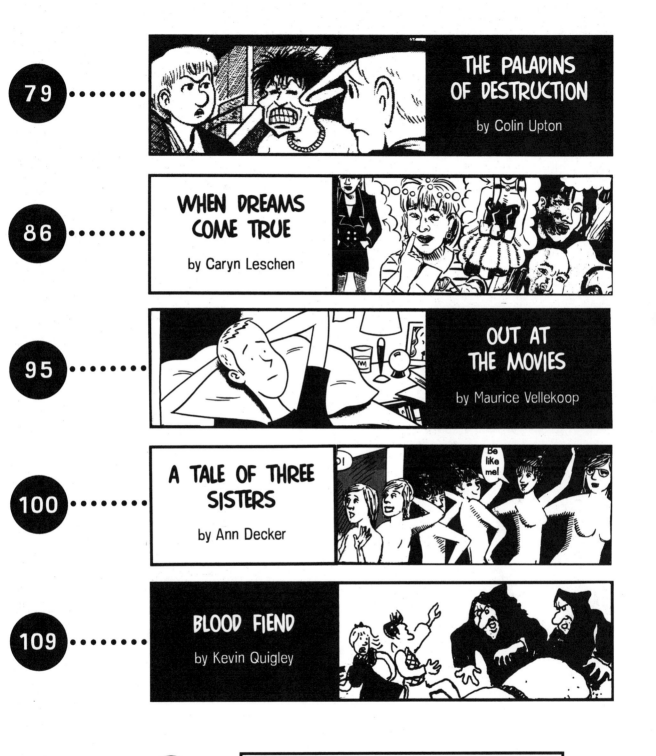

INTRODUCTION

So, just what *is* a Mind Riot, anyway? "Mind Riot" is an expression coined by ice climbers to describe a phenomenon whereby, at a critical juncture in a climb, the brain basically short-circuits. Faced with a hairy, potentially life-threatening situation, the climber checks the ropes, the gear, moves made, all avenues in and out. Then the climber checks everything again. And again—until he is, for all intents and purposes, paralyzed by his own thoughts. That's a Mind Riot. But what does it have to do with comix or adolescence?

Like ice climbing, surviving adolescence can be a grueling ordeal, filled with both exhilaration and misery. During the teenage years, the circuitry between mind and body often feels mis-wired. The various pressures exerted from family, friends, the media, conscience, hormones, and ego can tie a person up in knots. The result: another form of Mind Riot.

"Mind Riot" also suits the comic form. My discovery of so-called "alternative" comix when I was a teenager blew *my* mind—and my perception of what the genre could be. I knew about comics-with-a-"c": the yellowed Archie and Spiderman digests kept at my grandmother's house to entertain us kids while the grown-ups did their thing. I had long since outgrown those rags, and so I assumed, all comics. But while working in a mall bookstore during high school, I dis-covered—and was completely captivated by—Alan Moore and Dave Gibbon's *The Watchmen,* a dark response to the superhero genre, and *Maus,* art spiegelman's provocative, wrenching comic about how his father survived the Holocaust, and how he survived his father. Here, in both these works, was something completely different: comix-with-an-"x," comix with intelli-gence and attitude and the hard, black edge I didn't even know I had been looking for. Reading these books was, for me, a profoundly visceral experience. And I wasn't alone in this assess-ment. In his fascinating book, *Understanding Comics,* Scott McCloud bears witness to his love of the form, and dissects its unique and complex language. McCloud says—and I heartily agree—that comics are much more than the "crude, poorly-drawn, semiliterate, cheap, dispos-able kiddie fare" that so many of us are exposed to at an early age. At their best, with their intricate weaving of image and text, their "dance of the visible and invisible," they possess all the power and beauty of what we call art. I certainly was hooked, and over the next several years, ventured into a universe of high-quality, off-the-beaten-track comix.

• • •

It is from this ever-widening universe that the artists in *Mind Riot* hail. Since the beginning of the comix movement in the 1960s, many artists have taken coming-of-age as their subject. Those were the comix I loved best, with their gritty, honest, and often hilarious portraits of a time of life too often put in a soft-focus haze by the mainstream media. Then, while working as a children's book editor, I began to imagine comix not only *about* teenagers, but *for* them, speaking to young adults about their own lives. I approached artists whose work I admired and asked each of them to create an original story for the project, and slowly *Mind Riot* took shape. This collection is not by any means all-inclusive; there are many talented artists whose work, for lack of space and relative narrowness of topic, is not represented here. For those readers already familiar with comix, I hope *Mind Riot* broadens your perceptions of the form. For those new to comix, I hope you'll explore on your own. A resource list at the end of the book provides purchasing information and suggestions for further reading.

A few necessary words of gratitude. It was a privilege and a true pleasure to work with the artists in this book; I admire both their craft and their dedication to it. Thanks to all the people who lent me support, advice, and enthusiasm while I put *Mind Riot* together, including Frances Foster, Anne Schwartz, Ann Bobco, Ethan Trask, Kristin Lang, Lisa Harbin, and my folks. Thanks also to David Olson, without whom this book might have been titled *Untitled*. I am especially grateful to Peter Bagge, whose comic *Hate*, a chronicle of post-teenage life, is one of my all-time favorites. And last, but far from least, a resounding "gracias" to Ruth Katcher, my brave and tireless editor at Simon & Schuster. I couldn't have done this without you.

—KAREN D. HIRSCH

Before I was even a teenager, my idea of what it was like to be one was shaped by TV. Of course, what I witnessed there was a very glamorized version; casting directors seek to put on the screen the prettiest and most charming specimens of "teenage-hood," not the most realistic. But I contributed to my own misconceptions by seeing what I *wanted* to see: the teenage world as one completely separate from that of adults. In this world, *everyone* looked good, dressed sharp, listened to rock-n-roll, went on "swingin' dates," or simply drove around all day in search of that mythical party-that-never-ends. I assumed that teenagers always owned their own cars and never had to answer to their parents for anything. And so, my Burning Ambition when I was eight years old was to be a teenager *forever*.

Needless to say, by the time I turned thirteen I had a completely different outlook on the years that lay ahead of me. Undersized, underweight, with greasy, unruly hair to match my hideous acne, there was no way I was ever going to be the "swingin' teen" I once imagined myself becoming. How was I ever gonna go on a date when I could barely even squeak out a "hello" to a member of the opposite sex? At night, I lay in bed convinced that I would explode if I didn't lose my virginity by my next birthday, while my waking hours were spent predicting my imminent death from a brain tumor that had yet to materialize. In short, I was miserable.

Fortunately for me, I found an outlet in humor. When I was a teenager in the early 1970s, entertainment media, such as Woody Allen's movies, TV shows like *All in the Family,* and *National Lampoon*—style magazines, were becoming much more open and "reality-based" than they had been previously. This went a long way in relieving me of the feeling that I was the most miserable, alienated person on earth. These more honest forms of humor not only helped me realize that I wasn't the first or only person claiming that title, but also helped me connect with all the other Most-Miserable-Persons-on-Earth™. And, just as importantly, they helped me learn to laugh at myself and put my so-called problems in perspective. Meanwhile, though unbeknownst to me at the time, similar changes in humor and attitude were happening in comics. Having been raised on *MAD* magazine and daily cartoons such as *Peanuts,* I felt like I had outgrown that stuff, and the only comics I had access to that I found the least bit inspiring were the strips—Gahan Wilson's *Nuts,* for one—that ran in the back pages of the *Lampoon.* Superhero comics—then as now—depressed the hell out of me, since their sole purpose seemed to be to completely remove their readers from a reality that must have been even worse than mine; otherwise, why would those comics try so thoroughly to *escape* it, rather than to *deal* with it or even *laugh* at it? And I won't even talk about Archie comics, those shameless panderers of teenage myths! (Though I must admit, they were always good for an unintentional laugh.)

It wasn't until years later, after I had left my hometown and moved to the big city, that I discovered easy access to what were then known as "underground" comics, most notable for their psychedelic graphics, dope-smokin' humor, and hair-raisingly pornographic imagery. Yet, while I certainly was amused by all of the above qualities, the works that intrigued me most were the comics of a much more personal, autobiographical nature, such as those by Justin Green and Robert Crumb. These artists were unafraid to spell out, in the most brutally honest yet hilarious way imaginable, every twisted, neurotic sexual and/or religious hang-up suffered during adolescence. The effect of these comics on their readers was both immediate and cathartic, and they inspired many fellow cartoonists, from Matt Groenig (*The Simpsons*) to Lynda Barry (*Ernie Pook's Comeek*), not to mention many other lesser known, but no less talented, artists.

Women cartoonists in particular seemed, then and now, to be the most compelled to use comics in a highly personal way—almost like a diary—as you can plainly see in this collection, and in others, as well, most notably the *Twisted Sisters* anthologies. So strong is the temptation—the need, even—to tell all, that making a living has become secondary to simply expressing one's self. These days, many "alternative" (as we are now called) cartoonists have to earn money some other way, even if it means waiting tables or flipping burgers, and work on their comics during off hours, just as poets and painters always have. Such obsessiveness, usually with little profit to show for it, may not sound like a lot of fun (because it isn't!), but at least artists feel like they are making their mark through one of the most powerful forms of communication: comics. And their efforts leave the rest of us with a body of work to savor—like the work in *Mind Riot*, which I hope you can all relate to as much as I did. In fact, I think this book should be subtitled: *I Was Forced to Live the Life of a Teenager for Seven Years and Lived to Tell About It!*

—PETER BAGGE
SEATTLE, 1996

IDA MARX BLUE SPRUCE

Ida (pronounced Eeda) Marx Blue Spruce is a native New Yorker, and has been reading and drawing cartoons since childhood. She became more serious about comics after seeing the work of George Herriman, art spiegelman, and other greats in the field.

During her tumultuous teenage years, the New York City public schools finally drove her to the point of quitting high school at age 16.

She lived in the Woodstock, New York, area for a while, and then returned to New York City at age 25 to attend the School of Visual Arts until she graduated in 1988.

Ida now lives in Silver Spring, Maryland, just outside Washington, D.C., with her husband, Duane, and two-year-old son, Miles.

Her work has appeared in the *New Yorker, Drawn & Quarterly, Pictopia* (a Fantagraphics publication), the *Brooklyn Free Press,* and the *New Asian Times.*

SO, YOU'RE A CARTOONIST! WHY DON'T YOU DO YOUR NEXT BOOK REPORT IN CARTOON FORMAT!

I NEEDED A GOOD TEACHER IN THAT CRAZY YEAR. MY BEST FRIEND LIZ WASN'T IN ANY OF MY CLASSES.

HOW COME ALL THE OTHER KIDS SEEM TO KNOW EACH OTHER?

HA-HA-HA-

WHEN I FOUND MY FRIEND LORNA, SHE WAS WITH HER NEW HIGH SCHOOL FRIENDS.

OH, LORNA! HI!

WHO'S THAT, LORNA?

I HAVE NO IDEA.

HOW COULD YOU JUST COMPLETELY IGNORE SOMEONE WHO HAD BEEN YOUR FRIEND SINCE 4TH GRADE??

ULP.

WELL? YA WANT PITATIZ OR NOT?

I GOT THIS REALLY BIG LUMP IN MY THROAT AND COULDN'T TALK FOR MAYBE 20 MINUTES.

THEN, ON TOP OF ALREADY HATING SCHOOL, THIS GANG OF GIRLS ATTACKED ME IN THE SCHOOL YARD FOR NO REASON.

SMACK

YANK

I BEGGED MY MOTHER NOT TO MAKE ME GO BACK TO SCHOOL AFTER THAT, BUT SHE DID.

I STARTED TO FEEL AFRAID ALL THE TIME.

GLENN HEAD

When I was a kid of about thirteen, I walked into a head-shop called "Penny Lane." It had plenty of the stuff I was into: posters, blacklights, incense burners, etc. All the usual hippie paraphernalia for slumming middle-class kids like myself. One wall of the store, however, was something totally different: underground comics.

An eyeball orgy. That's the only way I can describe those comics. Sweating, straining, pulsating, vomiting—sometimes all on the same page! My eyes were throbbing. They still are. Reading the comics was even better. Sex, death, horror, banality, it was all there—including humor! All for the price of a comic book!

What I try to do with my comics is tell a good story. Along with that, I attempt to create a unique universe for my cartoon characters to walk around in. Hopefully it's inviting to the reader, but not safe. Reading a good comic strip should be like taking a skateboard down a treacherous hill at forty miles an hour. Do you take the risk and keep reading, or bail out before the gravel pit at the bottom of the hill? The choice is yours.

GREENBERGER/ROHRER

Dean Rohrer and David Greenberger began collaborating in 1992 when they produced the first chapter of *The Last Years of Arthur Wallace*. The protagonist of those stories and the one which follows here is based on an actual man by the name of Arthur Wallace, who lived his actual life in Boston (1893-1980). His appearance, as drawn by Dean, originates from the few existing photos of the man; his manner of speech, behavior, and attitudes have their basis in his relationship with David which was formed during Arthur's final year when he was living in the nursing home in which David then worked. Numerous installments of this saga have appeared in the comic book *Duplex Planet Illustrated*.

Dean Rohrer's comic drawings have appeared in the *New Yorker, Harpers, Details, Spy,* and numerous other periodicals. Additionally, his work has been featured on award-winning book and record covers. Dean lives with his wife and daughter outside Philadelphia.

David Greenberger has been exploring issues of aging and decline (as well as our culture's avoidance of the subject) since he started publishing *The Duplex Planet* in 1979. Since then, the ruminations, conversations, and interviews which fill its pages have been collected into books and CDs, performed as monologues, been the source of two films, and adapted into comic books and a play. David lives in New York State with his wife and daughter.

For more information on any of the work mentioned above, send a SASE to: The Duplex Planet, P.O. Box 1230, Saratoga Springs, NY 12866.

DIANE NOOMIN

Diane Noomin, creator of the infamous cartoon character DiDi Glitz, has been living and working in the Bay Area since 1973.

Her work has appeared in numerous comic books, magazines, and anthologies, including *Twisted Sisters 2: Drawing the Line* (Kitchen Sink Press, 1995), *Twisted Sisters: A Collection of Bad Girl Art* (Penguin USA, 1991), *The New Comics Anthology*, *The Nation*, *Art Forum*, and *SF Weekly*. She's also contributed to alternative magazines and comic books such as *The Nose*, *Weirdo*, *Young Lust*, *Wimmin's Comix*, and *True Glitz*.

In 1980 *I'd Rather Be Doing Something Else: The DiDi Glitz Story,* an original musical comedy, was produced in San Francisco.

Ms. Noomin has also curated several shows. White Columns Gallery in New York City, The Cartoon Art Museum of San Francisco, and La Luz de Jesus Gallery in Los Angeles have all had shows exhibiting her original art.

From Jawbreakers to Lawbreaker

A True Tale of a Teenage Thief

Stealing snuck up on me. The first time, I stole some money from my mother's purse...

WELCOME TO FANTASY ISLAND...

...and treated the entire second grade to jaw breakers!!

Me next!! I want a red one.

No! Me next. Quit shoving.

Joanie,* you can have a red one and a blue one!

Jill... you can be next!

POPULAR AT LAST!

* MOST POPULAR GIRL IN CLASS WITH PERFECT TURNED-UP NOSE

I got caught, of course... no candy for a long time!!

I just got a call, Diane... from Mrs. Edwards... it seems Joanie broke a tooth on a jaw breaker you gave her today. Just where did you get the money to—?

um... I um... found a five-dollar bill... in your purse...

RING

yes, Mrs. McClean... Jill broke a tooth... yes... I see—

Later on, I began to steal loose change from my Dad's overcoat pocket. I'd sneak downstairs in the early morning and try not to jingle the coins too loudly....

Jeez, Louise.... It's mostly pennies!!

When I turned 13 I stole a girdle from my Mom...

Next thing I know I'm explaining these ink blots and trying to psych out this shrink so he doesn't tell my parents I'm a nut case...

Turns out my folks are _much_ more freaked out about me cutting up my Mom's girdle than the loose change I'd snatched...

If they'd only _asked_ me, I could've told 'em it _wasn't_ hostility at all... just fear of flab!!

In junior high my Mom wouldn't let me wear makeup so I put it on in school and sneaked it off before she came home...

My pitiful allowance didn't begin to cover makeup so I started to steal- lipstick from a friend's Mom... eyeliner from an older cousin... nail polish from my Aunt Rita...

(within panels)

Perfect!! Now my butt is squeezed so tight it can't jiggle! I'll just trim this extra piece off...

It's only a cigar, right, Doc?

Does she hate me so much she's gotta mutilate my lingerie?

She's just asking for love.

I knew it! Those guys are laughin' at my jiggle-butt!!

Hey, babe... lookin' good!

phewt... phew...

mmph... ha...

Uh-oh—these eyelashes won't come off!!

Maybe I shouldn't have used Elmer's?

What're you doin' in there so long? Did ya fall in? Di-ane!!

I'll be right out...

My secret beauty stash grew until the fateful day I stole a can of hair spray from the neighbor I baby-sat for...

Yes, Mrs. Gluck... you're missing a new can of Allnet? Yes, I'll ask Diane if she's seen it!!

I decided it was safer and much less embarrassing to steal from strangers...

Here's your hair spray, Mrs. Gluck. I'm totally sorry.... I don't know why I took it — I guess I was having a bad hair day...

Gimme that, you little...

So at 14 I graduated to shoplifting. My friends and I liked Woolworth's best.

No thanks

Can I help you?

We'll just help ourselves...

3.99

One of our favorite techniques was to hold up an earring, pretend to check it out in the mirror and then pop it in our mouths.

Afterward, I'd look at the dumb earring and wonder why I did it...

Ecyew... I'm bleeding! I think I pierced my cheek!!

Cool!!

Once, my friend Nicole and I got caught stealing tapes, but we were too stupid to be afraid. The security guards were really pissed...

All right, kid... what's your name?

Paula Abdul... ha ha ha.

Ha ha. Janet Jackson.

?!

They knew we were goofin' on them, but they let us go for some reason....

And then Nicole got caught stealing a gold chain!!

Hold it right there, young lady! What's that in your pocket?

What gold chain?

She got sent to Juvenile Hall—

Dear Diane... it's way scary here... some of the girls have secret knives! I can't wait to get out! I miss you... I'd kill for a pizza...

No way I'm ending up there!! I haven't stolen anything in 3 months.

You need any help with the dishes, Ma?

... or I could fold the laundry...

I could get a head start on my term paper on the internal combustion engine...

Still, every time I pass by the makeup counter at Woolworth's my heart pounds!

oooh... Mocha Magic— my favorite!

MAYBELLINE 2 FOR 1 SALE!!

99¢

Last time, I ran out of there so fast a guard chased after me and searched my backpack...

I'm sorry Miss... my mistake!

It's okay.

Now, I'm looking for a part-time job.... Maybe Woolworth's is hiring!!

I wonder if there's an employee discount?

PERSONNEL

NOTICE

FOR SALE

Diane Noomin END

PHOEBE GLOECKNER

I think the reason I do cartoons of any kind now is because I saw some very good ones in my adolescence, a time when I was open to exploring new modes of expression for my teenage *malheur*. I never liked comic books particularly up until that point, but when I first saw the work of such artists as R. Crumb, Aline Kominsky, and Diane Noomin, I saw the possibilities of the medium and was truly inspired. My dad was an artist who died at a somewhat early age of causes related to the dicey "bohemian" lifestyle he led. Fears of ending up the same way led me to pursue a master's degree in medical illustration, with the hope of ensuring for myself the possibility of earning a livelihood. And now, indeed, I am a medical illustrator.

I work at home in a charming little studio with deep-red walls, half submerged in the slope of a steep hill covered with pine trees, albeit in the middle of a big West Coast city. But my walls are covered with layouts for comics I'm working on, and I steal the time whenever I can to get them a bit closer to completion.

VICKY RABINOWICZ

Growing up, Vicky dreamed of exploring the universe in search of interesting life-forms, but when she turned thirteen, her thoughts turned to clothes, makeup, and boys. These thoughts continued to plague her throughout her teenage years. Fortunately, as time passed, her interests expanded to include life, liberty, and the pursuit of happiness. But every so often her thoughts return to those of her youth, and, as she ponders the existence of UFOs, she might also wonder, "How does my butt look in these jeans?"

CAROL SWAIN

I was born in 1962, near London.

I studied painting at art school for four years, and began drawing comics in 1988. Originally I self-published my comic *Way Out Strips!* From 1992 it was published first by Tragedy Strikes Press in Canada, and then by Fantagraphics in the United States. In 1996 Fantagraphics published *Invasion of the Mind Sappers,* a seventy-two-page comic story.

My work's been published in Germany, Italy, France, Spain, Switzerland, Portugal, Finland, Sweden, and Japan.

I have work in the Cartoon Art Museum in San Francisco and on the Internet.

My teenage years were spent in rural Wales, a long way from big-city life. It was the sort of place where people had to make their own entertainment. You just had to be sure you weren't the main feature.

I'd moved there from a big city, so I was an outsider, like my near neighbor—the farmer with his painted friends.

Painted friends

Before

After

CAROL TYLER

In high school my hair was rolled every night with huge orange juice cans to get a sleek under-curve (Sassoon didn't exist yet). I suffered constant neck pains from sleeping on those dopey things. My struggle to eliminate one solid eyebrow was constant. Without weekly tweezing, I looked like a defensive linebacker. Eye shadow? Blue/green, of course, with black eye-liner and mascara. The braces finally came off my sophomore year, but my chipped, pointy front teeth continued to frighten.

My high school had girls on one side, boys on the other, which made any chance at a social life grim. To help the dating effort, my friends on the girls' side decided to nominate me for homecoming queen. This was the time for all my beauty efforts to pay off. I felt popular that week . . . until the election. The boys thought I was a bowzer and I got like two votes from their side. What was wrong with me? One thing was certain: The makeup rituals had to go.

Ten years later, at my high school reunion, those same boys—disco dudes all—approached me apologetically, proclaiming basically the same thing: "I really wanted to go out wit chew but I thought Joe would beat da krap outta me." You see, my older brother Joe was the greatest athletic legend ever to happen at Carmel High School in Mundelein, Illinois. He was a god. Even though he graduated after my freshman year, his residual aura continued to emanate from trophies and retired jerseys! Thank god for reunions. But just as my self-esteem was restored, this one guy, Frank, said to me, ". . . So was it true that you wore a football helmet to bed every night to keep your hair straight?"

PETER KUPER

Peter Kuper was raised by wolves and spent his early years drawing on cave walls. As an adult, his scrawls appear in a wide variety of magazines and newspapers when he's not busy howling at the moon.

THE END

ROBERTA GREGORY

Roberta Gregory has been writing and drawing comics all her life, and though she has a loyal following and has gotten much critical acclaim, she has managed to retain her obscurity. The comic book medium is still largely male-dominated, and some years she has been virtually the only female creator to get nominations in the Eisner industry awards. Fortunately more and more young women are discovering the possibilities in this unique creative medium, and are becoming readers and creators, so things *can* change!

Roberta's first story was published in 1974, and in 1976 she became the first woman to solo self-publish a comic book, *Dynamite Damsels*. Since then she has produced hundreds of pages, self-published two books and two more comics, and is now best known for her long-running series, *Naughty Bits*, from Fantagraphics Books. She also has an ongoing series published in Germany, and after more than twenty years is finally making a humble living solely from her sense of humor and ability to draw funny pictures, so she's glad she stuck with it!

COLIN UPTON

Colin Upton is a resident of Vancouver, British Columbia, a city he loves passionately. He lives there with his cat, Walrus, who receives her own fan mail.

While growing up, Colin was ruined forever as a productive citizen by Monty Python, punk rock, and comics by Herge (the creator of *Tin Tin*).

After dropping out of art school, poverty, unemployment, and boredom inspired him to create his first mini-comic in a friend's basement. Over the next five years he made more than 60 mini-comics and digests before the first *Colin Upton's Big Thing* was published in 1990. Four more *Big Things* were published by Fantagraphics, and another by Aeon; Starhead released *The Big Black Thing*, a comic based on a prank.

Colin's work is primarily autobiographical, although his interests range from urban fiction to humor to fantasy to politics and history, as well as random mixtures of the above. Public transit is a particularly rich source of material. His work has appeared in numerous comics anthologies, several gallery shows, comic conventions in Europe, and in local papers, including a regular review of comic books in the *Vancouver Review*. He recently released a new series, *Buddha on the Road*, an adventure/religious satire. He also bowls, plays drums in the band Puke Theatre, and is a founding member of the performance group The Haters.

Write Colin for a free catalog at 6424 Chester Street, Vancouver, British Columbia, Canada V5W 3C3.

CARYN LESCHEN

Caryn was a miserable, exceptionally tall preteen with a big nose, from the farthest reaches of outer Queens, New York. She secretly wanted to go to the California College of Arts & Crafts after high school, but assumed it was too far away & too expensive & her parents would never go for it. She managed to look & feel quite gawky clear through to her late twenties, when she got hit by a bolt of lightning & realized that, if nothing else, she HAD to go to art school so she could learn how to dress. After slinging countless cappucinos & balancing miles of dinner plates up her arm in both New York & San Francisco, she finally put herself through the California College of Arts & Crafts, where she learned not only how to wear only black, but also how to draw hands faster.

Caryn sees comix as little movies where you get to say what you want & control everything. She is the creator of *Ask Aunt Violet*, America's funniest & deepest advice cartoon, which appears almost weekly in lots of cool papers such as *The SF Weekly* & *The Chicago Reader*. She is also a book & magazine illustrator, & loves getting paid to draw & paint, even though the stress makes her eat too many pretzels. In 1996 Caryn was hired to create an online soap opera, *Pthalo Ptheatre*, where she tosses the details of her own life into a blender & serves them up as entertainment, just like she does with her comics.

Caryn's advice to teens is: Don't be afraid to ask your parents for what you really want, even if you think they'll never go for it. Only you can really make your dreams come true, & you've got to start somewhere.

MAURICE VELLEKOOP

When I was a teenager in the late '70s, my big sister was really the only person in the world I felt I could bare my soul to. My high school was a very homophobic place in which to experience my awakening sexuality. Like Gary in my story "Out at the Movies," I spent a lot of time on my own, in front of the TV watching the *Late Show* or at the local repertory cinema with my sister. Movies definitely were an escape from our humdrum suburban surroundings, but they also suggested the rich possibilities life might have in store for us.

In the story, Gary has a supportive group of friends, and meets a fun, outspoken young lesbian. His first coming-out experience is a positive one. I'd like to think that most young people today find it easier to come to terms with what it means to be gay than I did. I suspect, though, that there are still many gay teens out there struggling with their fears and oppression. I certainly couldn't have made it through those years without the movies, and, more importantly, without my sister and friend. Ingrid, this story is for you!

Maurice Vellekoop lives on Ward's Island in Toronto with his cat, Fred.

OUT at the MOVIES

by Maurice Vellekoop

Wow! Barbara Stanwyck is SO incredible! They just don't make movie stars like her anymore.

CINEMATHEQUE PRESENTS: FILMS of the '40s

If only Rick and Rosie and Jake were into this kinda stuff. Man, we'd be like a team! They'd come with me to film school and we'd make the coolest stuff together!

Me and Jake get off on all the same music and Rick and I agree on books sometimes but we all seem to part ways at the movie theater... and, boy, when it comes to romance we're on different planets! I betcha Rick and Rosie end up together.

They seem so sure of themselves. My sexlife takes place purely in my imagination... If only I could talk to them about stuff.

Hi, Mum. Hi, Dad.

How can I confide what I'm not even sure of myself? I KNOW I'd rather date Robert Taylor than Liz Taylor, but how can you make up your mind about what you've never tried? I've never even kissed a girl, let alone another guy.

ANN DECKER

I grew up in Baltimore in the 1950s, the youngest of three sisters. This story is loosely based on events from my childhood.

From the outside, my family probably seemed perfect—but I didn't even feel close to normal. Intense anxieties kept me awake at night. As an adolescent, I was angry and alienated and did everything I could to rebel. I flunked and cut classes, bleached my hair, got caught stealing, hung out with tough kids, and snuck boys home while my parents were out. Everyone thought I would become a juvenile delinquent.

After I left home, I began to see that my sisters and mother had their own troubles. We were all struggling with so-called "ideals" of femininity. But instead of supporting each other, we were competitive and critical. And we didn't know how to talk about what was happening to us.

As I grew older, I learned that the problems I had in those years weren't mine alone. Our culture is permeated with petty values and unrealistic expectations for how women should look, feel, and act. It's hard to grow up!

My purpose in doing this story was to give something to girls who are struggling and think the obstacles they face are in their heads. Maybe so, but those obstacles are also in the world.

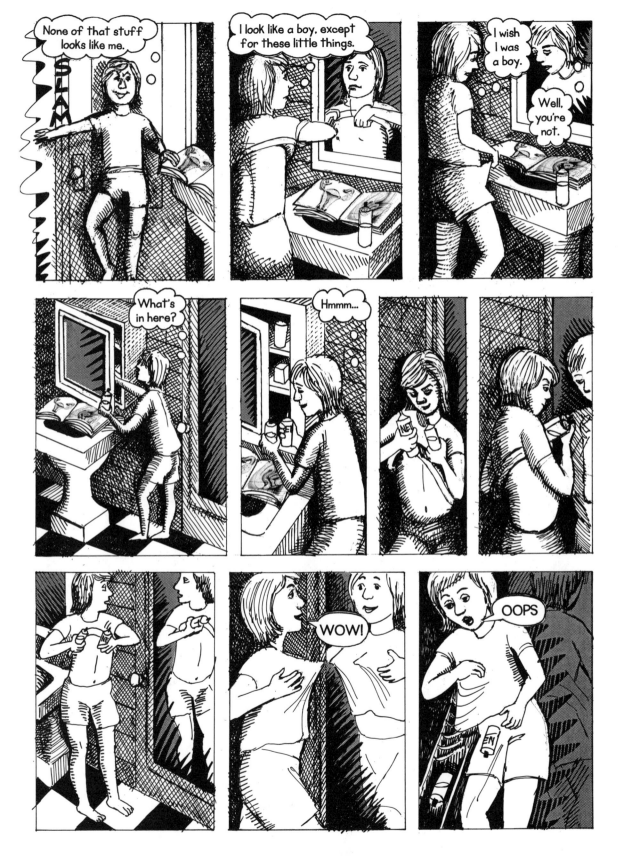

THE FIRST MOVIE KEVIN QUIGLEY SAW IN A THEATER WAS *IN SEARCH OF THE CASTAWAYS*, FEATURING HAYLEY MILLS. HE INSTANTLY FELL IN LOVE WITH THE GREAT STAR, AN OBSESSION LASTING THROUGH MOST OF THE 1960'S, AND ONLY SERIOUSLY RIVALED WHEN, IN THE FIFTH GRADE, HE FELL FOR *BETTY* AND *VERONICA*. PLAGUED BY ALLERGIES, QUIGLEY SNIFFLED AND DRIPPED HIS WAY THROUGH HIGH SCHOOL ON LONG ISLAND. STILL, HE WONDERED WHY HE DIDN'T HAVE A GIRLFRIEND. HE LIVED, FOR MANY YEARS, IN BINGHAMTON NEW YORK, RARELY SNEEZING. HE NOW LIVES IN SOUTH JERSEY, WITH HIS WIFE AND DAUGHTER, AND THE ALLERGIES ARE BACK. NEVERTHELESS, HE CONTINUES TO CUT THE GRASS REGULARLY...

K.Q. 1996

BLOOD FIEND

RESOURCES FOR COMIX FANS

Local comic shops are likely to have the widest selection of "alternative" comix. But as comix increase in popularity, bookstores are getting in on the act: Check their magazine, science fiction, and humor sections, or ask a clerk. Some really cool stores might even have a special section for comix and graphic novels. Ask the stores to be sure to stock your favorite comix, and encourage your library to order comix in book form; you have the power to influence what they carry! Ordering by mail directly from comix publishers and distributors is another option. Be forewarned, however, that due to the explicit nature of some comix, they may not be available to readers under the age of eighteen.

SELECTED BIBLIOGRAPHY

Here is a brief and highly subjective list of good comix anthologies, magazines, and seminal works.

BOOKS ABOUT COMIX

Comics and Sequential Art by Will Eisner (Poorhouse Press). One of the first books to examine the comic form, by an early and great comic artist.

Understanding Comics by Scott McCloud (Kitchen Sink Press). A brief history and ambitious definition of comics, in comic form.

COMIX ANTHOLOGIES

The Best Comix of the Decade (Vol. 1 & 2) selected by the editors of *The Comics Journal* (Fantagraphics). A wide selection of comix published between 1980 and 1990.

The Best of Drawn & Quarterly (Vol. 1 & 2). Stories collected from the first ten issues of the comix magazine, many in full color.

Twisted Sisters: A Collection of Bad Girl Art and ***Twisted Sisters 2: Drawing the Line*** edited by Diane Noomin (Penguin). Two anthologies of hard-hitting comix by women. Also available as a comic book published by Kitchen Sink Press.

World War III Illustrated edited by Peter Kuper and Seth Tobocman (Fantagraphics). Selections from the first ten issues of the long-running political comic journal.

COMIX IN BOOK FORM

Maus (Vol. 1 & 2) by art spiegelman (Pantheon). A comic about the Holocaust and families, with mice and cats as protagonists. Winner of the Pulitzer Prize.

Neon Lit edited by Bob Callahan (Avon). A series of novels adapted into comic form. Published titles include *City of Glass* by Paul Auster, drawn by David Mazzuchelli, and *Perdita Durango* by Barry Gifford, drawn by Scott Gillis.

The Watchmen by Alan Moore, drawn by Dave Gibbons (DC Comics). Originally published in comic form, then as a graphic novel. Bridges the gap between comix and more mainstream superhero comics.

COMIX MAGAZINES AND COMIX COLLECTIONS IN MAGAZINE FORM

There are many collections of comix published both regularly and irregularly in magazine form. Some of my favorites include *Drawn & Quarterly, Girltalk, Snake Eyes,* and *Twisted Sisters.* Local comic book and 'zine shops may carry lesser-known, self-published mini-comics. *Factsheet Five* provides information and reviews of a host of small 'zines, including comics. The *Comics Journal* is a monthly magazine with strong coverage of the comix scene.

COMIX PUBLISHERS WITH MAIL-ORDER CATALOGS:

Cat Head Comix
P.O. Box 576
Hudson, MA 01749

Kitchen Sink Press
320 Riverside Dr.
Northampton, MA 01060

Drawn & Quarterly Publications
5550 Jeanne Mance St., #16
Quebec, Canada H2V 4K6

Last Gasp Eco-Funnies, Inc.
777 Florida St.
San Francisco, CA 94110

Fantagraphics Books
7563 Lake City Way N.E.
Seattle, WA 98115

Rip Off Press, Inc.
P.O. Box 4686
Auburn, CA 95604

COMIX ON THE WEB

The World Wide Web is the most recent and rapidly expanding venue for comix. There is a staggering amount of material on-line for both fans and creators alike. I've listed some of my favorite comix-oriented web-sites. Be forewarned that some of these pages may not exist by the time you read this; web "homes" are notoriously ephemeral, and many of the best sites are created by college kids who have an annoying tendency to graduate and abandon their web projects. And lots of new sites will come into existence after the compilation of this list.

A good place to start looking for other web pages is the directory maintained by Yahoo (www.yahoo.com) or other search engines. A search for either "comics" or "comix" should turn up enough pages to keep you occupied for weeks.

Cat-Head Comics Institute (world.std.com/~cathead) publishes lots of "happenin' comics." Their site has product information and links to other comix pages.

Fantagraphics (www.eden.com/comics/fantagraphics.html) is one of the largest and most professional alternative comix sites, run by one of the largest and most professional alternative-comix publishers.

Independent Comics (grove.ufl.edu/~jrm/independent.html), ***Comics World*** (www.farrsite.com/cw/index.html), ***Comix Reviews*** (weber.u.washington.edu/~keb/comix.rev.html) and ***Necron Underground Comix*** (www.vol.it/necron) provide a plethora of information and reviews about comix around the world.

Wow Cool (www.eden.com/wowcool/wowcool.html) is a great source for lesser-known comix and 'zines.

Indy Magazine (grove.ufl.edu/~jrm), ***Comics Journal*** (www.halcyon.com/fgraphic/home.html), and ***Comics Magazine*** (members.aol.com/comicszine/index.html) are on-line magazines that cater, at least in part, to readers of alternative comix.

Alternative Comix WWW Guide (copper.ucs.indiana.edu/~mfragass/altcom.html) helps guide you through the land of cyber-comix.

Small Press Zone (www.cloudnet.com/~hamlinck/spz.htm) and ***Small Press Comic FAQ*** (www.sentext.net/~sardine/spfaq.html) are idiosyncratic sites geared towards creators of alternative comix.

Friends of Lulu (nspace.cts.com/Lulu/) is an organization dedicated to the inclusion and involvement of women and girls in comics.

Comic Book Legal Defense Fund (www.insu.com/cbdlf) is a non-profit organization which protects comic book creators and publishers against censorship.

The only currently active Usenet newsgroup that I know of dedicated to the discussion of alternative comix is (rec.arts.comics.alternative). Check it out; it's a nifty group.